For Paul
(who took me back to school)
and to all the children and teachers,
past and present, who have made
my times at Langley School so special,
with warmest love

And also to Plymbridge Woods nearby

First published 1993 by Walker Books Ltd
87 Vauxhall Walk, London SE11 5HJ

This edition published 1995

6 8 10 9 7 5

Printed in Hong Kong/China

This book has been typeset in Bembo.

British Library Cataloguing in Publication Data
A catalogue record for this book is available
from the British Library.
ISBN 0-7445-3661-8

THIS WALKER BOOK BELONGS TO:

_____

_____

_____

_____

The WILD WOODS

SIMON JAMES

WALKER BOOKS
AND SUBSIDIARIES
LONDON • BOSTON • SYDNEY

Jess and her grandad saw
a squirrel one day, down by
the Wild Woods.
"I'd like to take him home,"
Jess said.

"You can't keep a squirrel,"
cried Grandad.
"They're too wild."

"Don't worry Grandad," said Jess,
"I'll look after him."
"But Jess," called Grandad,
"you can't keep a squirrel.
  What are you going to feed him?"

"He likes our sandwiches,"
Jess said.

"But Jess, come back!" shouted Grandad.
"You can't keep a squirrel.
  Where's he going to sleep?"

"I'll make him a bed in
my room," Jess said.

"Hurry up, Grandad!" said Jess.
"Come and see. I think I've
found a waterfall."

"Jess, you can't really keep a
   squirrel," whispered Grandad.
"I know," said Jess.
"He belongs to the wild."

"I love being in the wild,"
Jess said. "Can we come
back tomorrow?"
"Well… OK," sighed Grandad.
"If we really have to."
"Good," Jess said, "because …

one of those
ducks might need
looking after."

MORE WALKER PAPERBACKS
For You to Enjoy

Also by Simon James

SALLY AND THE LIMPET

An unusual "green" tale about a girl who disturbs
a limpet and finds it's stuck to her finger.

"A gentle, thoughtful story with wonderful illustrations."
Practical Parenting

0-7445-2020-7   £4.99

MY FRIEND WHALE

The moving story of a boy and the whale with whom he plays
each night. Then one sad night the whale does not come…

"A lovely, gentle picture book with beautiful,
blue illustrations." *Practical Parenting*

0-7445-2349-4   £4.99

DEAR GREENPEACE

"One of the best books of the year, taking the form of letters
between a small girl and Greenpeace, to which she writes for
advice about a whale she finds in her garden pond…
A perfect book for 3 to 5-year-olds."
Valerie Bierman, The Scotsman

0-7445-3060-1   £4.99